D0551574

CHILDREN'S
STORYTIME COLLECTION

The Lonely Mermaid

AND OTHER STORIES

Contents

The Lonely Mermaid

There once lived a mermaid named Miriam who was very lonely. All day long she sat on a rock combing her long, yellow hair and singing to herself. Sometimes she would flick her beautiful turquoise fish tail in the water and watch the ripples spreading far out to sea. Miriam had not always been lonely. In fact, she used to have a pair of playmates called Octopus and Dolphin. Octopus had gone off to another part of the ocean to work for the Sea King. He was always much in demand because he could do eight jobs at once – one with each arm. Dolphin, meanwhile, had gone away to teach singing in a school of dolphins. Miriam once thought she heard his lovely song far away across the ocean and she hoped in vain that he might come back and play.

One day Miriam was sitting on her favourite rock as usual. "How lonely I am," she sighed to her reflection as she combed her hair and gazed at herself in the mirror.

To her astonishment, her reflection seemed to answer back. "Don't be lonely," said a voice. "Come and play with me."

Miriam couldn't understand it at all. She peered into the mirror and then she saw, beyond her own reflection, another mermaid! She was so startled that she dropped the mirror and her comb and spun around.

Miriam was puzzled by the sight in front of her. For there, sitting on the next rock was another mermaid – and yet she didn't look like a mermaid in many ways. She had short, dark, curly hair and wore a strange costume that definitely wasn't made of seaweed. When Miriam looked down to where the mermaid's fish tail should have been, she wanted to burst out laughing.

For instead of a beautiful tail, the other mermaid had two strange limbs like an extra long pair of arms stretching down.

The other 'mermaid', who was really a little girl called Georgie, was equally amazed by the sight of Miriam. She had seen pictures of mermaids in books before, but now she couldn't quite believe her eyes. For here, on the rock beside her, was a real live mermaid!

For a moment they were both too astonished to speak. Then they both said at once, "Who are you?"

"I'm Miriam," said Miriam.

"I'm Georgie," said Georgie.

"Let's go for a swim," said Miriam. Soon the two of them were in the water, chasing each other and giggling.

"Let's play tag along the beach," suggested Georgie, and started swimming towards the shore. She had quite forgotten that Miriam would not be able to run around on dry land. Miriam followed though she was rather afraid, as her mother had always told her not to go near the shore in case she got stranded. Georgie ran out of the water and up on to the beach.

"Wait for me!" called Miriam, struggling in the water as her tail thrashed about. Then, to her astonishment, something strange happened. She found she could leave the water with ease and, looking down, saw that her tail had disappeared and that in its place were two of those strange long arm things like Georgie's.

"What's happened?" she wailed.

Georgie looked round. "You've grown legs!" she shouted in amazement. "Now you can play tag!"

Miriam found that she rather liked having legs. She tried jumping in the air, and Georgie taught her to hop and skip. "You can come and stay at my house, but first I must find you some clothes," said Georgie, looking at Miriam who was wearing nothing but her long, yellow hair. "Wait for me here!"

Georgie ran off and soon she was back with a tee shirt and shorts. Miriam put them on. They ran back to Georgie's house together. "This is my friend Miriam," said Georgie to her mother. "Can she stay for tea?"

"Why, of course," said Georgie's mother.

"What's that strange thing?" whispered Miriam.

"It's a chair," said Georgie. She showed Miriam how to sit on the chair. All through teatime Miriam watched Georgie to see how she should eat from a plate and drink from a cup and saucer. She'd never tasted food like this before. How she wished she could have chocolate cake at home under the sea!

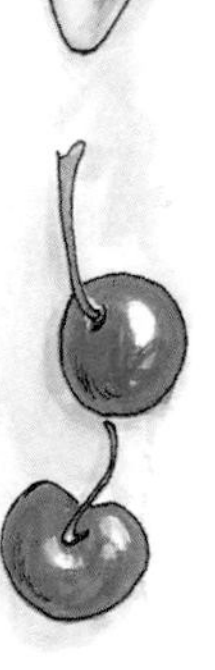

After tea Miriam said, "Now I'll show *you* how to do something." Taking Georgie by the hand she led her down to the beach again. There they picked up shells, and then Miriam showed Georgie how to make a lovely necklace from shells threaded with seaweed. While they made their necklaces, Miriam taught Georgie how to sing songs of the sea.

Soon it was bedtime. "You can sleep in the spare bed in my room," said Georgie. Miriam slipped in between the sheets. How strange it felt! She was used to feeling water all around her and here she was lying in a bed. She tossed and turned, feeling hotter and hotter, and couldn't sleep at all. In the middle of the night she got up and threw open the window to get some fresh air.

She could smell the salty sea air and she began to feel rather homesick. Then she heard a familiar sound from far away. It was Dolphin calling to her! The noise was getting closer and closer until at last Miriam knew what she must do. She slipped out of the house and ran down to the beach in the moonlight. As soon as her toes touched the water, her legs turned back into a fish tail and she swam out to sea to join Dolphin.

The next morning, when Georgie woke up, she was very upset to find that her friend had gone. When she told her mother who Miriam really was, her mother said, "The sea is a mermaid's true home and that's where she belongs. But I'm sure you two will always be friends."

And indeed, from time to time, Georgie was sure that she could see Miriam waving to her from the sea.

The Ugly Duckling

Once upon a time, there was a mother duck who laid a clutch of six beautiful little eggs. One day, she looked into her nest in amazement. For there were her six small eggs but lying next to them was another egg that was much, much bigger than the others. "That's odd," she thought, and went back to sitting on the nest.

Soon, one by one, the smaller eggs hatched, and out came six pretty yellow ducklings. Yet the bigger egg still had not hatched.

The mother duck sat on the large egg for another day and another night until eventually the egg cracked, and out tumbled a seventh duckling.

But this one was very different. He was big, with scruffy grey feathers and large brown feet.

"You do look different from my other chicks," exclaimed the mother duck, "but never mind, I'm sure you've got a heart of gold." And she cuddled him to her with all the other ducklings. Sure enough, he was very sweet-natured and happily played alongside the other ducklings.

One day, the mother duck led her ducklings down to the river to learn to swim. One by one they jumped into the water and splashed about. But when the big grey duckling leaped into the water he swam beautifully. He could swim faster and further than any of his brothers or sisters. The other ducklings were jealous and began to resent him.

"You're a big ugly duckling," they hissed at him. "You don't belong here." And when their mother wasn't looking they chased him right away.

The ugly duckling felt very sad as he waddled away across the fields. "I know I'm not fluffy and golden like my brothers and sisters," he said to himself. "I may have scruffy grey feathers and big brown feet, but I'm just as good as they are – and I'm better at swimming!" He sat down under a bush and started to cry. Just then he heard a terrible sound – CRACK! CRACK! It was the sound of a gun. There were men out there shooting ducks. Then, only a short way from where he was hiding, a dog rushed past him, sniffing the ground. The ugly duckling did not dare to move. He stayed under the bush until it was dark and only then did he feel it was safe to come out.

He set off, not knowing which way he was going until eventually, through the darkness, he saw a light shining. The light came from a cosy-looking cottage. The ugly duckling looked inside cautiously. He could see a fire burning in the hearth and sitting by the fire was an old woman with a hen and a cat.

"Come in, little duckling," said the old woman. "You are welcome to stay here. For now I can have duck's eggs each day as well as hen's eggs."

The ugly duckling was glad to warm himself by the fire. When the old lady had gone to bed, the hen and the cat cornered the duckling.

"Can you lay eggs?" enquired the hen.

"No," replied the duckling.

"Can you catch mice?" demanded the cat.

"No," replied the miserable duckling.

"Well, you're no use then, are you?" they sneered.

The next day, the old woman scolded the duckling: "You've been here a whole day and not one egg! You're no use, are you?"

So the ugly duckling waddled off out of the cottage. "I know when I'm not wanted," he said to himself mournfully.

He wandered along for a very long time until at last he reached a lake where he could live without anyone to bother him. He lived on the lake for many months. Gradually the days got shorter and the nights longer. The wind blew the leaves off the trees. Winter came and the weather turned bitterly cold. The lake froze over and the ugly duckling shivered under the reeds at the lake's edge. He was desperately cold, hungry and lonely, but he had nowhere else to go.

At last spring came, the weather got warmer and the ice on the lake melted. The ugly duckling felt the sun on his feathers. "I think I'll go for a swim," he thought. He swam right out into the middle of the lake, where the water was as clear as a mirror. He looked down at his reflection in the water and stared and stared. Staring back at him was a beautiful white bird with a long, elegant neck. "I'm no longer an ugly duckling," he said to himself, "but what am I?"

At that moment three big white birds just like himself flew towards him and landed on the lake. They swam right up to him and one of them said, "You are the handsomest swan that we have ever seen. Would you care to join us?"

"So *that's* what I am – I'm a swan," thought the bird that had been an ugly duckling. "I would love to join you," he said to the other swans. "Am I really a swan?" he asked, not quite believing it could be true.

"Of course you are!" replied the others. "Can't you see you're just like us?"

The three older swans became his best friends and the ugly duckling, that was now a beautiful swan, swam across the lake with them and there they lived together. He knew that he was one of them and that he would never be lonely again.

No Hunting!

Mr Rabbit opened his eyes and gave a big yawn. He thought it seemed like the perfect day for going outside and nibbling some of the farmer's lettuces. And after that he thought he would go and see how well the farmer's carrots were growing, and maybe have a little nibble of those as well. He popped his head out of his burrow and looked this way and that, in case he saw any danger. Then he pricked up his ears and turned this way and that, in case he heard any danger. Finally, he sniffed the air this way and that, in case he smelled any danger. It seemed safe, so he hopped out of his burrow.

No sooner had he gone a couple of steps when "ZING" – a bullet whizzed past his head. Mr Rabbit jumped back into his burrow as fast as he could go, shaking with fright.

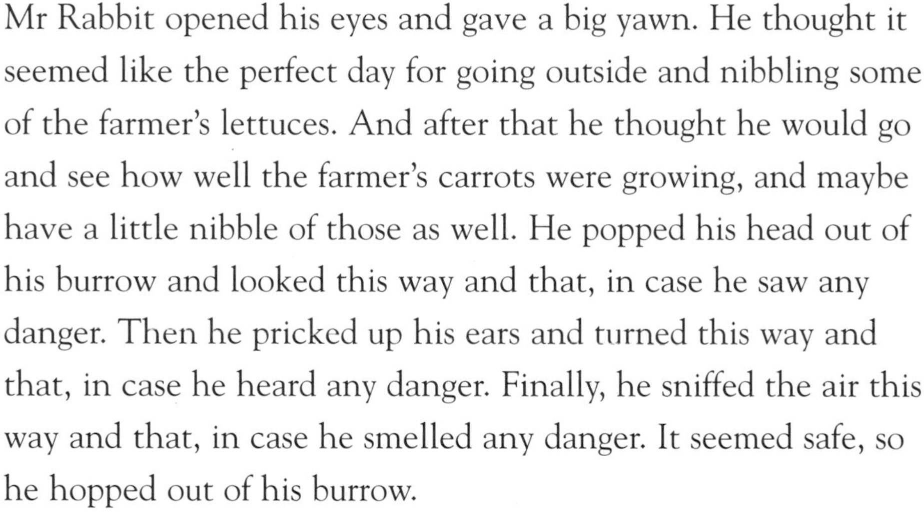

"Goodness, it's the rabbit hunting season," he gasped. He gathered his family of young rabbits around him and spoke to them. "Now children, listen very carefully," he said. "The rabbit hunting season has begun, so you must all stay safely inside the burrow until it's over. I will go out at night and forage for food for us all."

His children looked at him in dismay. "But it's lovely and sunny outside," they cried all together. "We'll be very careful."

But Mr Rabbit was having none of it. He insisted that they all stay under ground until the rabbit season was over.

For a few days, the young rabbits amused themselves as best they could by playing chase and hide and seek. But they were becoming very bored. Finally, they decided that they were going to do something to stop the rabbit hunting themselves.

First Tom, the eldest of Mr Rabbit's children, decided he would try and stop the hunters. So when it was dark, he crept out of the burrow and made his way towards the hunters' hut.

Although it was night and he was sure the hunters would be asleep, he was still very scared. Soon he came to the hut. It was standing in a clearing in the woods. It was dark inside the hut and he hoped the hunters were asleep. “If I can dig some big holes,” he thought, “maybe they will fall into them in the morning and won’t be able to get out until the hunting season is over.”

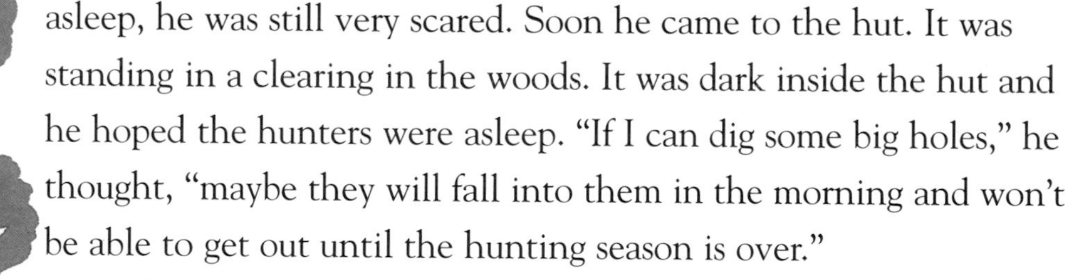

So he dug and he dug like he had never dug before. Soon there were holes everywhere, right outside the door to the hunters’ hut. Feeling very pleased with himself, but also very tired, Tom made his way back to the burrow just before it was light.

When the hunters awoke, they went straight out without falling down a single hole! Poor Tom, he had dug lots of holes alright, but the hunters’ hut had two doors, and the hunters had simply gone out of the other one!

Then Jenny, the second oldest of Mr Rabbit's children, decided that she would try and stop the hunters. So when it was dark, she crept out of the burrow and made her way towards the hunters' hut. When she got there, she noticed that the window was open and so she decided to go inside. She, too, was very scared, but she thought about having to spend all those days in the burrow until the hunting season was over and that gave her the courage to carry on.

Inside the hut, she could see the hunters sleeping in their beds. She looked around, wondering what she could do to stop them hunting. Then suddenly she saw the hunters' clothes lying on a chair. Quick as a flash, she hopped up to them and started nibbling at them. In no time at all, the clothes were in shreds. "That'll stop them," thought Jenny. "They can't hunt without their clothes on!" Satisfied with her night's work, Jenny made her way back to the burrow just as dawn was breaking.

When the hunters awoke, they got straight up and went out hunting! Poor Jenny, she had chewed some clothes alright, but she had only chewed some spare clothes! The hunters had gone to bed wearing their other clothes in order to be out quickly in the morning.

Finally, Penelope, the youngest of Mr Rabbit's children, said she would try and stop the hunters.

"Don't be silly," said Tom to his sister. "You are far too young to be going out at night."

"And anyway," said Jenny, "what could you possibly think of doing to stop the hunters?"

"I'll think of something," said Penelope, who was really quite a clever little rabbit.

So that night, she crept out of the burrow and made her way to the hunters' hut. The window was open, just as before, and so Penelope hopped inside. She looked on the floor, she looked in the cupboards, and she looked under the beds, but she couldn't think of anything to stop the hunters.

Then she looked up and suddenly had an idea. For there on the table was a calendar, showing that very day's date. Penelope hopped on to the table and started to turn the pages. Finally she came to a page on the calendar that read: "RABBIT HUNTING SEASON ENDS TODAY". Satisfied with her work, Penelope hopped out of the hunters' hut and back home to her burrow.

In the morning, the hunters woke up, rubbed their eyes and got out of their beds. One of them glanced at the calendar. "Oh no!" he suddenly exclaimed. "Look at the date! The rabbit hunting season is over."

With that, the hunters (who were too silly to realise that someone else must have turned over the pages of the calendar) packed their belongings and went home. All was peace and quiet once more and the rabbits could hop about in the open air in safety.

The Mirror of Dreams

The house on the corner of Nightingale Avenue was tall and very handsome, and was by far the largest in the neighbourhood. From the street you could see four floors of beautifully decorated rooms, and if you peeped over the railings you could see the basement below. If you were lucky enough to be asked into the house, and passed through the beautiful hallways into the playroom, you might meet the owner's daughter, Cordelia. Sometimes Cordelia would be sitting in her silk pyjamas playing on her grand piano, and sometimes she would be dressed in the finest velvet gowns playing with her lovely dolls.

If you went down the stairs and into the basement, you might come across Polly. Polly's mother was a chambermaid in the house, and worked hard all day long to make the house sparkling clean. Sometimes Polly helped her to polish the ornaments and dust the furniture, but more often Polly sat on her own in her small bedroom drawing pictures with some crayons on a drawing pad she had been given for her birthday. When Polly was helping to polish the furniture she would look longingly at all of

Cordelia's fine clothes and toys, and when she sat alone in her room she would draw pictures of all the beautiful things she would like to own if only she could afford them.

One day, a large parcel was delivered to the house and taken upstairs to Cordelia's bedroom. A little while later, Cordelia's maid carried a pretty, ornate mirror down from her room and put it with the rubbish waiting for collection outside the house. Polly asked the maid why the mirror was to be thrown away, and the maid explained that Cordelia had been given a new mirror in which to brush her long, silky locks, and that she didn't need it any more. The maid then asked if Polly would like the old mirror, and of course Polly accepted with pleasure – it was the most beautiful thing she had ever owned.

Polly carried the mirror back to her room and polished it lovingly. As she polished the glass a strange thing started to happen. The glass went misty, and then cleared as her own reflection stared back at her once more. But the reflection that stared back was not dressed in rags and worn old clothes as Polly was, but in a rich gown of the most beautiful cream satin, with pink bows and apricot lace.

Polly was entranced. She looked almost as beautiful as Cordelia! Her hair gleamed and her fingers were white and magnificent. As she looked further into the mirror, she saw herself dancing at a ball, and then sitting down to eat the finest food she had ever seen – hams and roasted meats, and cakes of strawberries and cream!

And then the mirror spoke to her. "I am the Mirror of Dreams," the cool, clear voice said. "Whatever your heart desires most will be reflected in my shiny surface."

Polly was astounded, but so happy. She didn't care that it was only a day dream, for when she saw her reflection in the beautiful clothes, she felt as if she were truly there dancing and eating the fine foods – she could almost taste the fruit and cream in her mouth!

From that day on, Polly sat in her room every day, and dreamed and dreamed and dreamed. She had never felt so happy before, and could not wait to wake up each morning to visit her imaginary world. She certainly didn't understand how Cordelia

could have thrown away such a magical wonder, and thought that she could not have known of its enchanting secret. She supposed also that Cordelia could have had no use for such a mirror, for whatever Cordelia wanted in real life she received, and would have no need to dream. But Polly was to find out that this was very far from true!

Weeks passed, and every day Polly sat and dreamed of ermine cloaks, of diamonds and pearls, of parties and picnics and carnivals. Eventually, she had dreamed every dream she had ever wanted. And Polly began to realise that it no longer made her as happy as it once had, and she began to grow weary of her Mirror of Dreams. She sat in front of the mirror less and less, and eventually when she did visit the mirror she could not think of a single thing that would make her happy. Even the dreams she had in which her mother wore fine silk clothes and didn't have to scrub and clean for their living could no longer make her happy.

She preferred her real mother, who came to kiss her good night and read her stories no matter how tired and overworked she was. Eventually she stopped looking in the mirror altogether, and finally decided to throw the mirror away – it had only made her more unhappy.

As the long winter turned into spring she acted upon her decision, and took down the mirror to throw away with the rubbish. But as she looked into the glass, it misted over in its familiar way and she saw herself in the mirror as she looked in real life, but in it she was playing with other children like herself, and reading stories with them and sharing toys. She felt gloriously happy, and knew in that instant that all she wanted was a very good friend. She realised in that moment, too, that perhaps Cordelia really had known the mirror's secret, but that she also had become more unhappy as the dreams faded and reality forced itself upon her. She wondered aloud what it was that Cordelia had dreamed of, and for the second and last time the mirror spoke in its cool, clear voice.

"The Mirror of Dreams showed Cordelia her heart's desire, and her heart desires a true friend and companion – someone who is not jealous of her wealth, but a friend who will share her hopes and dreams, and with whom she can have parties, games and picnics."

Polly put the mirror down and thought with amazement that she could be that friend, if Cordelia would be friends with someone poor but honest and true. Polly left the mirror with the household rubbish and was about to make the descent back to the basement, when she saw Cordelia standing in the garden at the back of the house. Cordelia had seen her discard the mirror, and shyly walked up to Polly. Polly overcame her shyness also and went to meet Cordelia, and then she told her they shared the same dream.

Cordelia and Polly became the best of friends from that day on. They shared everything they had, no matter how much or little. They talked and laughed together all day long, and they played long into the evening. They didn't have to dream any more, for they had both got their true heart's desire.

Goldilocks and the Three Bears

There once lived a little girl who had long, golden hair. Because of this, everyone knew her as Goldilocks. Goldilocks and her mother lived together in a cosy little cottage in the forest.

"Would you like some pretty flowers?" Goldilocks asked her mother one day. "I will pick you some if you like."

"That would be lovely, my dear," said her mother. "But mind you don't get lost. Don't stray too far, and don't be too long."

Goldilocks gave her mother a big hug and promised to be careful. She picked up her little flower basket and skipped off into the forest to look for flowers.

First she came upon some big, bright daffodils. She picked a few and placed them in her basket. A little further on, she spied some pretty bluebells and so she picked a bunch of those as well. Then she saw, even further on, some lovely marigolds which she also picked and put into her basket.

Well, Goldilocks was so busy picking all these wonderful flowers that she wandered further and further into the forest. Suddenly she realised that she was lost. She didn't know which way to turn. She was also beginning to feel very hungry and tired.

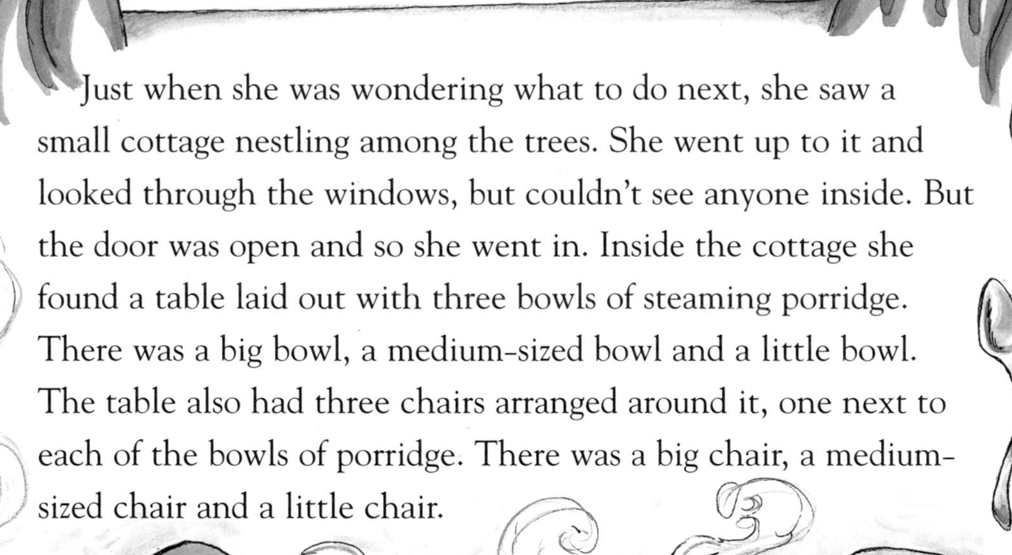

Just when she was wondering what to do next, she saw a small cottage nestling among the trees. She went up to it and looked through the windows, but couldn't see anyone inside. But the door was open and so she went in. Inside the cottage she found a table laid out with three bowls of steaming porridge. There was a big bowl, a medium-sized bowl and a little bowl. The table also had three chairs arranged around it, one next to each of the bowls of porridge. There was a big chair, a medium-sized chair and a little chair.

Goldilocks was so tired that she simply had to sit down. First she sat down in the big chair, but it was very hard and lumpy. It wasn't comfortable at all. Then she tried the medium-sized chair, but that didn't feel comfortable either. At last, she tried the little chair, but as soon as she sat down in it – it broke! She was too heavy for the little chair. "Oh dear," thought Goldilocks.

Instead of sitting down, she thought she would have some porridge as she was still very hungry. First she took a spoonful of porridge from the big bowl. But it was too hot, and so she couldn't eat it. Then she tried a spoonful from the medium-sized bowl, but it was too lumpy. So she tried a spoonful from the little bowl. And guess what? It tasted so delicious that she ate it all up!

"Oh, I do feel sleepy," yawned Goldilocks after she had finished the porridge in the little bowl. "I wonder if there is a nice, comfortable bed I can sleep in."

So she went upstairs and found a bedroom with three beds in it. There was a big bed, a medium-sized bed and a little bed. First she tried the big bed, but it was very hard and didn't feel comfortable at all. Next she tried the medium-sized bed, but it was too soft and that didn't feel comfortable either. Finally, she tried the little bed. It was just right – warm and cosy. Soon she was fast asleep.

Just then, the family of three bears who lived in the cottage came back from their walk in the forest. As soon as they came in through the front door, they knew someone had been there.

"Who has been sitting in my chair?" said Daddy Bear, in a deep, gruff voice.

"And who has been sitting in my chair?" asked Mummy Bear in a softer voice.

"Who has broken my chair?" cried Baby Bear in a squeaky voice.

Then the three bears looked on the table.

"Someone has been trying my porridge," said Daddy Bear.

"And someone has been trying my porridge, too," said Mummy Bear.

"Who has eaten all my porridge?" said Baby Bear, who by now was very upset and sobbing big tears.

Upstairs went the three bears and into their bedroom.

"Who has been sleeping in my bed?" asked Daddy Bear.

"And who has been sleeping in my bed?" asked Mummy Bear.

Suddenly, Baby Bear gave a cry of surprise. "Look!" he yelled. "There's someone sleeping in my bed."

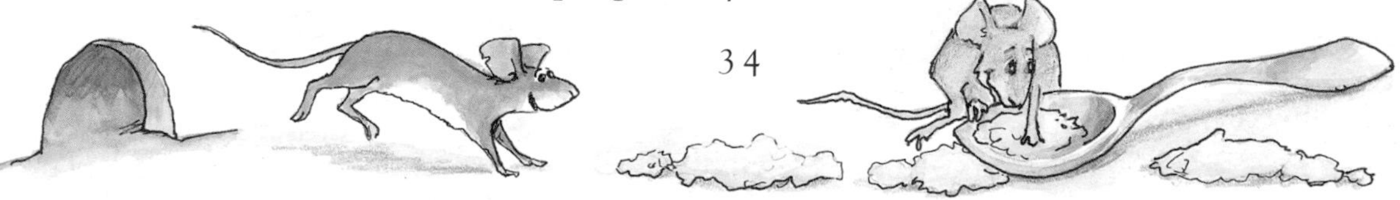

Goldilocks woke up with a start when she heard all the noise. She looked up to see the three bears staring down at her. She was so frightened that she jumped straight out of bed, down the stairs and out through the front door. Then she ran and ran until she arrived back home to her own cottage again.

And do you know, that was the last that the three bears ever saw of Goldilocks!

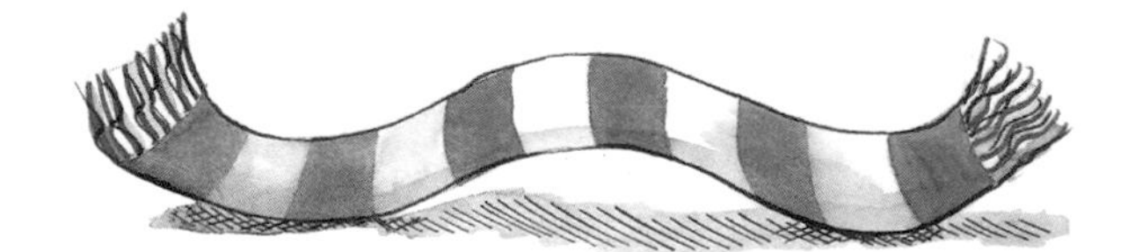

The Missing Scarf

Kanga was very proud of her stripy knitted scarf. She had made it herself and she had also made a smaller matching one for her son, Joey. Kanga used to hop through the bush with her scarf streaming out behind her, while Joey's could just be seen poking out of the top of her pouch. Now Joey was older, he was too big for Kanga's pouch, but he still wore his scarf as he hopped along beside his mother.

Then one day Kanga woke up to find that her beautiful scarf was missing. She searched high and low but it was nowhere to be found. Eventually she decided that she would have to go out into the bush to look for it.

"Stay here," she said to Joey. "I'll try not to be long. I'm sure to find my scarf soon." Kanga hopped off into the bush and started to search among the roots of trees and under stones.

She had gone quite a long way when, looking up into the branches of a eucalyptus tree, she spotted Koala. Now Koala was usually to be found asleep, but this time she was busy preparing a meal of eucalyptus leaves for her children. Kanga looked up at Koala and then her jaw dropped. For Koala was quite clearly wearing Kanga's scarf around her tummy. Then, to Kanga's horror, she saw Koala use the end of the scarf to wipe the teacups! "Koala," Kanga called. "Whatever do you think you're doing?"

Koala stopped cleaning the teacups and looked down through the branches of the eucalyptus tree at Kanga. "I'm wiping my teacups with my apron," she replied sleepily, "and I'll thank you not to interfere!" And with that, she yawned and moved several branches further up the tree.

Poor Kanga felt very embarrassed. How could she have mistaken Koala's striped apron for her own scarf? She hopped away and carried on further into the bush. After a while she could hear Kookaburra's familiar laughing call nearby. "I know," thought Kanga, "I'll ask her if she's seen my scarf. She'd be able to spot it easily from up in the sky." She followed the sound of Kookaburra's call until she came to the tree where she lived. She looked up and, sure enough, there was Kookaburra flying towards the tree. Kanga was about to call up when her jaw dropped again. For Kookaburra was quite clearly carrying Kanga's scarf in her beak. "Kookaburra," Kanga called. "Whatever do you think you're doing?"

"I'm lining my nest," mumbled Kookaburra through a beakful of stripy feathers. "And I'll thank you not to interfere," she added more distinctly, for she had now reached the nest and was arranging the feathers carefully in place.

Poor Kanga felt even more embarrassed. How could she have mistaken the feathers for her own scarf? She hopped away and carried on further into the bush. After a while she reached a wide open plain and there she saw Emu running past with his baby chicks on his back. As he rushed past, Kanga's jaw dropped yet again. For Emu quite clearly had Kanga's scarf tucked in among his chicks. "Emu," called Kanga. "Whatever do you think you're doing?"

"I'm taking my chicks to safety," said Emu, glancing up at the sky as he sped away. "And you'd be wise to do the same," he added. Then Kanga realised that what she had thought was her rolled-up scarf were just the striped chicks on Emu's back.

Poor Kanga felt even more embarrassed. How could she have made such a mistake? Then she felt a few spots of rain on her nose and, looking up, saw a huge black cloud overhead. There was no time to lose – she must find shelter.

She made a dash for some trees at the edge of the plain and soon found herself by a stream. She wandered along beside the stream feeling cold, wet, tired and miserable. Finally, she lay down in the wet grass beside the stream and tried to get to sleep. She shivered with cold and wondered how Joey was and whether he was behaving himself. She so hoped he hadn't got into mischief.

Just then there was a tap on her shoulder and there stood Platypus. "I could hear you in my burrow over there," she said pointing towards a hole beside the stream just above the water. "I thought you might like this to keep you warm," she added.

"My scarf!" exclaimed Kanga.

"Oh, is that what it is? I'm ever so sorry," said Platypus. "I've been using it as a blanket for my babies. It's rather cold and damp in my burrow, you know," she added, rather forlornly.

"Where did you find it?" asked Kanga.

"It was stuck on some thorns and I know I shouldn't have taken it, but I just thought it would be so nice for keeping my

young ones warm," blurted Platypus, and she started to sob.

"There now," said Kanga, "don't cry. You can keep the scarf. You need it more than me."

Platypus stopped crying and looked overjoyed. "Thank you," she said.

"No, thank you," said Kanga. "I've learned a lesson, which is not to get upset over a scarf, for I've ended up falling out with my friends."

Kanga made her way back home, but it took a long time because she apologised to all her friends on the way. When she explained what had happened Emu, Kookaburra and Koala all forgave her, and by the time she reached home she was feeling much better. Joey was there to greet her. "What have you been up to while I was away?" she asked.

"I made you this," he said. He handed her a scarf. It was a very funny-looking scarf, made out of twigs, grass and feathers, but Kanga loved it very much.

"This is much more special than my old scarf," she said. And she gave Joey an extra big hug.

Little Tim and His Brother Sam

Little Tim was a very lucky boy. He had a lovely home, with the nicest parents you could hope for. He had a big garden, with a swing and a football net in it. And growing in the garden were lots of trees that you could climb and have adventures in. Little Tim even had a nice school, which he enjoyed going to every day and where he had lots of friends. In fact, almost everything in Tim's life was nice. Everything that is apart from one thing – Tim's brother Sam.

Sam was a very naughty boy. Worse still, whenever he got into mischief – which he did almost all of the time – he managed to make it look as though someone else was to blame. And that someone was usually poor Tim!

Once Sam thought that he would put salt in the sugar bowl instead of sugar. That afternoon, Sam and Tim's parents had some friends round for tea. All the guests put salt in their cups of tea, of course, thinking it was sugar. Well, being very polite they didn't like to say anything, even though their cups of tea tasted very strange indeed! When Sam and Tim's parents tasted their tea, however, they guessed immediately that someone had been playing a trick. They had to apologise to their guests and make them all fresh cups of tea. And who got the blame? Little Tim did, because Sam had sprinkled salt on Tim's bedroom floor so that their mother would think that Tim was the culprit.

Another time, Sam and Tim were playing football in the garden when Sam accidentally kicked the ball against a window and broke it. Sam immediately ran away and hid, so that when their father came out to investigate, only Tim was to be seen. So poor little Tim got the blame again.

Then there was the time when Sam and Tim's Aunt Jessica came to stay. She was a very nice lady, but she hated anything creepy-crawly, and as far as she was concerned that included frogs. So what did Sam do? Why, he went down to the garden pond and got a big, green frog to put in Aunt Jessica's handbag. When Aunt Jessica opened her handbag to get her glasses out, there staring out of the bag at her were two froggy eyes.

"Croak!" said the frog.

"Eeek!" yelled Aunt Jessica and almost jumped out of her skin.

"I told Tim not to do it," said Sam.

Tim opened his mouth and was just about to protest his innocence when his mother said, "Tim, go to your room immediately and don't come out until you are told."

Poor Tim went to his room and had to stay there until after supper. Sam thought it was very funny.

The next day, Sam decided that he would play another prank and blame it on Tim. He went to the garden shed and, one by one, took out all the garden tools. When he thought no-one was watching, he hid them all in Tim's bedroom cupboard. In went the spade, the fork, the watering can, the trowel – in fact, everything except the lawnmower. And the only reason that the lawnmower didn't go in was because it was too heavy to carry!

But this time, Sam's little prank was about to come unstuck, for Aunt Jessica had seen him creeping up the stairs to Tim's bedroom with the garden tools. She guessed immediately what Sam was up to, and who was likely to get the blame. When Sam wasn't about, she spoke to Tim. The two of them whispered to each other for a few seconds and then smiled triumphantly.

Later that day, Sam and Tim's father went to the garden shed to do some gardening. Imagine his surprise when all he saw were some old flower pots and the lawnmower. He searched high and low for the garden tools. He looked behind the compost heap, under the garden steps, behind the sand pit and in the garage. But they weren't anywhere to be seen.

Then he started searching in the house. He looked in the kitchen cupboard, and was just looking under the stairs when something at the top of the stairs caught his eye. The handle from the garden spade was sticking out of the door to Sam's bedroom. Looking rather puzzled, he went upstairs and walked into Sam's bedroom. There, nestling neatly in the cupboard, were the rest of the tools.

"Sam, come up here immediately," called his father.

Sam, not realising anything was amiss, came sauntering upstairs. Suddenly he saw all the garden tools that he had so carefully hidden in Tim's cupboard now sitting in *his* cupboard. He was speechless.

"Right," said his father, "before you go out to play, you can take all the tools back down to the garden shed. Then you can cut the grass. Then you can dig over the flower beds, and then you can do the weeding."

Well, it took Sam hours to do all the gardening. Tim and Aunt Jessica watched from the window and clutched their sides with laughter. Sam never did find out how all the garden tools found their way into his bedroom, but I think you've guessed, haven't you?

This is a Parragon Book
This edition published in 2000

Parragon
Queen Street House
4 Queen Street
Bath BA1 1HE

Written by Derek Hall, Alison Morris and Louisa Somerville
Illustrated by Natalie Bould, Maureen Galvani, Virginia Margerison, Julia Oliver, Sara Silcock and Gillian Toft

Printed and bound in Spain
ISBN 0-75253-531-5